Sails, Pails and Alligator Tales

Fourth in the Georgia Series

Written by:
Rhonda Frost Petty

Illustrated by:
Pam Alexander

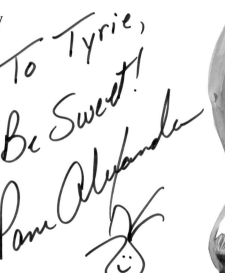

*To Tyrie,
Be Sweet!
Pam Alexander*

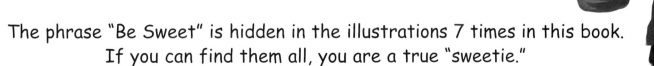

The phrase "Be Sweet" is hidden in the illustrations 7 times in this book.
If you can find them all, you are a true "sweetie."

A special thanks to Vance Buchan from Douglas, GA
for giving us the title for this book.

Rhonda, its been a wonderful five years. Thanks for being my partner and friend.
Love you, Pam

Text copyright ©2005
Illustrations copyright ©2005 by Pam Alexander

Printed in the U.S.A.

First U.S.Edition 2005

Yumion™ used by permission from the Toombs-Montgomery Chamber on Commerce.
Vidalia Onion® used by permission for the Georgia Department of Agriculture.

Published by Be Sweet Publications
ISBN 0-9709105-6-8

Website: www.besweetpublications.com

In Springtime in Helen,
a city so fair,
there's a festival of balloons
filled with hot air.

The Onion Ambassador
went to take in the view,
and he thought,
"From up there I could see something new!"

Yumion found a nice man who would give him a ride;
"Hop on in!" said the man, so he climbed up inside.

But a gust came along and the rope broke free.
Yumion looked down and cried, "Who'll rescue me?!"

The balloon was blown skyward up and away,
and in minutes Yumion floated over the U. of G-A!

Sanford Stadium is where the Dawgs "hunker down",
Yumion said, "I think Athens is the name of this town."

Another blast of the wind tossed Yumion around,
and he could see Rock Eagle there on the ground.

The 6,000 year old landmark was quite a site from the air;
it was awesome the Native Americans had built it there.

Again the wind shifted and the balloon again lifted,
and this time over Macon is where he then drifted.

The cherry blossoms in bloom were a beautiful sight.
There was so much to see on the astonishing flight!

The wind blew again in another direction,
over a place for which Georgians feel great affection.

Yumion knew that Savannah had much history,
like James Oglethorpe, Mary Musgrove, and Tomochichi.

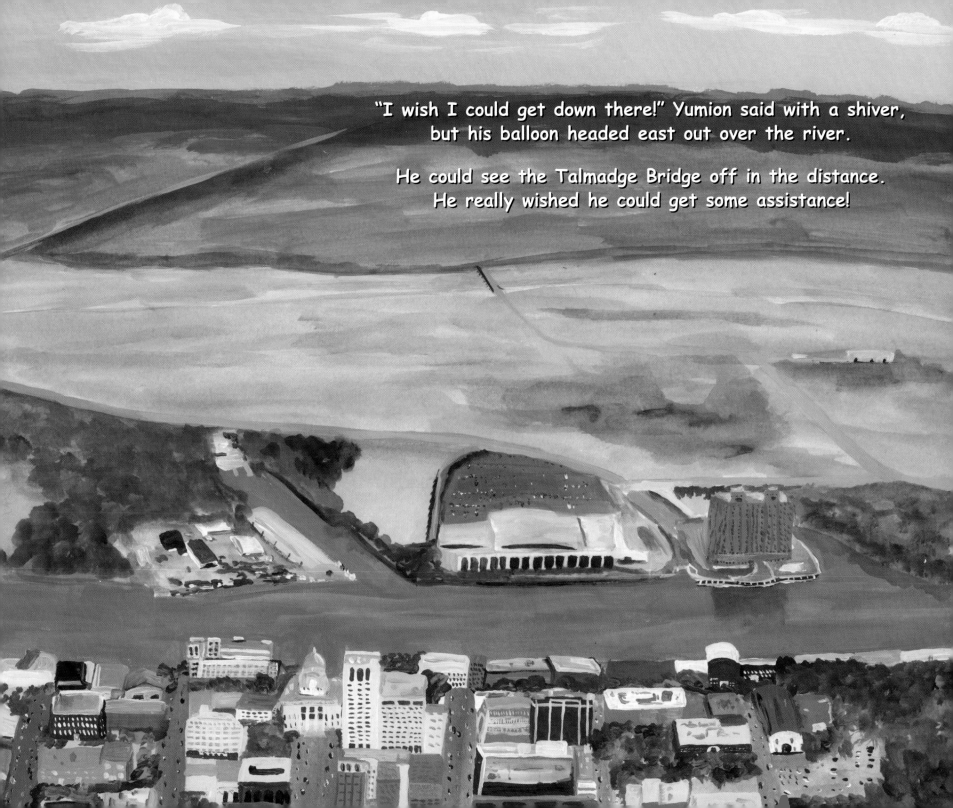

"I wish I could get down there!" Yumion said with a shiver,
but his balloon headed east out over the river.

He could see the Talmadge Bridge off in the distance.
He really wished he could get some assistance!

Although he saw much from this beautiful view, he couldn't get down. Oh, what could he do?!

"Yikes!" Yumion thought as the wind blew him faster! If he went over the ocean it would be a disaster!

Yumion shouted, "Please help me, it's almost too late!"
But the balloon snagged on the lighthouse and began to deflate!

He was on Tybee Island at the lovely seashore,
then new friends sent him inland so he could explore.

Back in Savannah, Yumion saw beautiful flowers;
statues and fountains, he could stay here for hours!

A carriage passed by on a cobble stoned walk.
Oh the tales they could tell if these oak trees could talk!

"They'd tell stories, I bet, of peacetime and war,
and of weddings and parties and so much more!"

There'd be so much to see if Yumion could stay,
but he continued his trip down the low country way.

Yumion had heard about shrimp boats with catches to boast,
but he hoped to learn about Georgia islands the most!

He got his wish as a boat docked at high tide.
The captain said, "Come aboard and I'll be your guide."

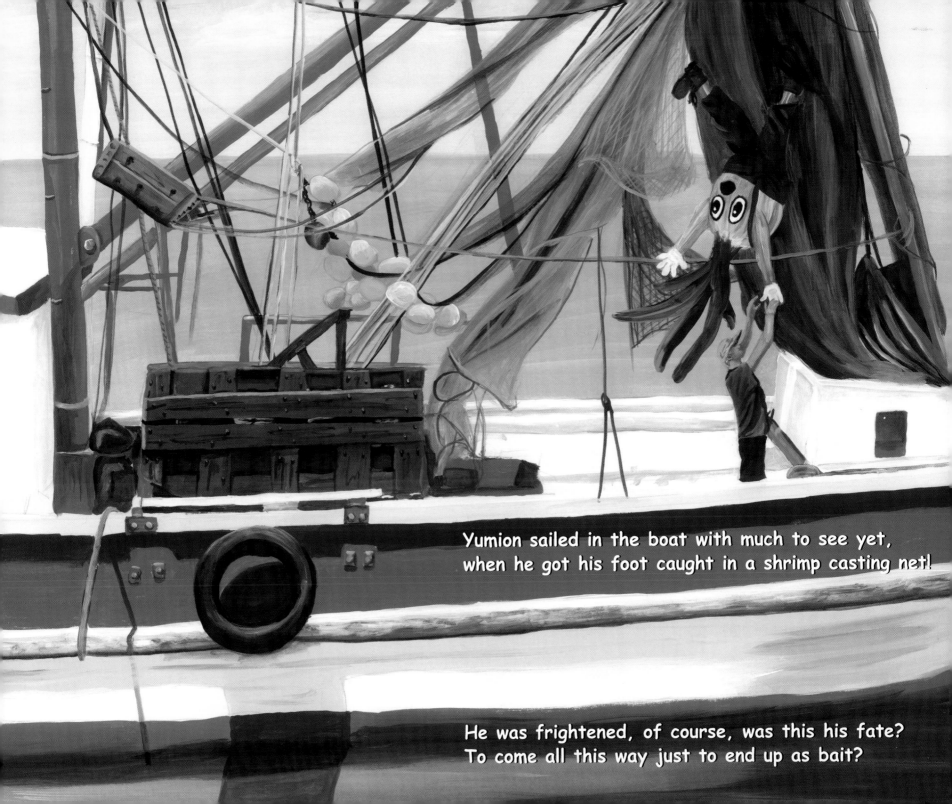

Yumion sailed in the boat with much to see yet,
when he got his foot caught in a shrimp casting net!

He was frightened, of course, was this his fate?
To come all this way just to end up as bait?

The shrimper helped Yumion out of his mess,
and said, "You're better on land than at sea I would guess,
so I'll take you to Sapelo Island with me,
we'll learn about a way of life called Geechee."

The people on the island were busy as bees;
giving tours, weaving baskets, and casting shrimp nets with ease.

He could easily stay here beneath mossy oaks,
but he had to visit more islands and meet more folks!

The isle of St. Simons was his next destination,
the place where lots of Georgians love to vacation!

He met some beachcombers and learned something new:
the crabs on the beach like sweet onions too!

Yumion looked around and tried to discover
a way of getting from one golden isle to another.

The bridge to the south was the Sidney Lanier,
it was the way to get to Jekyll Island from here.

Special laws keep Jekyll in its natural state,
and now that he was here he could hardly wait!

Yumion came here to see a unique island creature.
He'd heard about one that lays eggs on the beach here.

As he watched the waves and heard their roar,
a loggerhead turtle appeared on the shore.

Yumion said, "I can't believe my luck! This is grand!
She's coming up here to lay eggs in the sand!"

Yumion wanted to see Cumberland Island for sure,
and he could only get there on a ferry boat tour.

They floated by King's Bay's submarine ports,
and to his surprise, they had dolphin escorts!

He had never seen a more beautiful place!
From the dunes he looked out on the wide open space;
where fresh water meets salt and there are seashells galore.
He now knew why people loved the seashore.

Yumion was having such a wonderful time on the sand,
he forgot about the horses that inhabit this land.

A young horse wandered toward him away from the others,
but Yumion knew he shouldn't come between babies and mothers!

Yumion was loving these beachcombing days,
with nice ocean breezes and warm sunny rays.

He loved all the new stories that he had acquired,
but the sun going down made him suddenly tired!

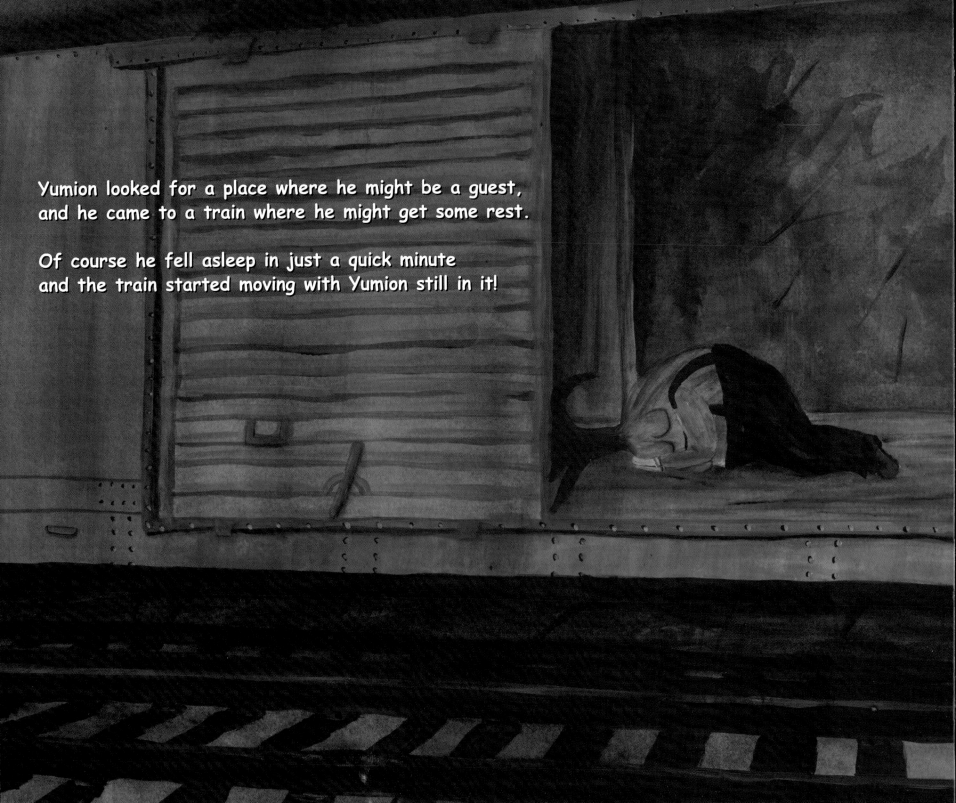

Yumion looked for a place where he might be a guest,
and he came to a train where he might get some rest.

Of course he fell asleep in just a quick minute
and the train started moving with Yumion still in it!

Yumion slept very soundly right there on the floor,
until they rounded a curve and he rolled out the door!

He hit the ground rolling and then to his surprise,
the place where he stopped was surrounded by eyes!

Yumion was frightened there alone in the night, especially when he saw a strange swinging light.

It was a man from the swamp and he said, "I'll be! What's a big onion doing in the Okeefenokee?"

They became friends quickly and went out to explore;
Yumion learned about rattlesnakes, orchids, and more.

The man told him stories of the swamp and its worth,
and how it was named "land of the trembling earth."

The stories of alligators were the ones he liked most.
A big male named Oscar is one about which they boast.

Yumion decided to get out of the boat for a rest,
but he was chased by a mother away from her nest!

Yumion's latest adventure had come to an end,
but we never can tell what's around the next bend.

A more well-traveled onion you never will meet;
just remember he told you to always BE SWEET!

Important Places and State Symbols in this book

 The state sea shell is the Knobbed Whelk.

 The Cherokee rose is the state flower.

The live oak is Georgia's state tree.

- The University of Georgia is the first state-chartered university in America by the Georgia General Assembly in January 17, 1785.

- Rock Eagle is an effigy mound found at the 4-H Conference Center in Eatonton, Georgia.

- Macon, Georgia is famous for many things including Mercer University, the Georgia Music Hall of Fame, and the Cherry Blossom Festival.

- Helen, Georgia is a replica of a Bavarian village in the mountains of north Georgia.

- Savannah was first established in 1733 by James Oglethorpe.

- African and American cultures blend to make Sapelo Island unique.

- Rich in history and beauty, St. Simons Island captures all.

- Only thirty percent of Jekyll Island can be developed in order to preserve its natural beauty.

- Cumberland Island is the largest natural wildlife preserve on the east coast of the United States.